To my first grandson, Jacob Albert Mann
A. G. H.

To Abbe and Jacob, and to my mom
M. S.

First edition 2003

Library of Congress Cataloging-in-Publication Data

Hines, Anna Grossnickle.
My grandma is coming to town / by Anna Grossnickle Hines ; illustrated by Melissa Sweet. — 1st ed.
p.   cm.
Summary: Albert and his grandma have a special long-distance relationship,
but when she comes to visit, it takes him a little while to overcome his shyness.
ISBN 0-7636-1237-5
[1. Grandmothers — Fiction.] I. Sweet, Melissa, ill. II. Title.
PZ7.H572 Myf 2003
[E] — dc21   00-049374

2 4 6 8 10 9 7 5 3 1

Printed in China

This book was typeset in Kidprint.
The illustrations were done in acrylic and colored pencil.

Candlewick Press
2067 Massachusetts Avenue
Cambridge, Massachusetts 02140

visit us at www.candlewick.com

My Grandma Is Coming to Town

Anna Grossnickle Hines

illustrated by Melissa Sweet

CANDLEWICK PRESS
CAMBRIDGE, MASSACHUSETTS

My grandma lives far away.

When I was a baby, she came to see me.

She taught me

"Pat-a-cake, pat-a-cake, baker's man,
Roll it and pat it, and put it in a pan."

I could only say, "Patta patta, rolla rolla."

Now I can say all the words, but when Grandma calls on the phone, she still says, "Patta patta."
"Rolla rolla," I say.
It is our special way of saying hello. I like to play that telephone game with Grandma.

I have pictures of my Pat-a-Cake Grandma
and she has pictures of me.

She sends me the best surprises . . .
like my rhyme book and Nosey.
She said Nosey could give me nose kisses.
Nose kisses make me laugh.

Pat-a-Cake Grandma lives too far away to give me real kisses and hugs, so she puts lots of X kisses and O hugs in her letters. I send her X kisses, too.

Last week she sent me a letter that said
she was coming to see me. I can hardly wait.

Dear Albert,
　　Hark, hark, the dogs
do bark,
　　Your Grandma is
coming to town.
　　She'll fly in a great
big airplane,
　　Up in the air and down.
　　　　Love,
　　　　　grandma
XOXOXOOOXOXO

I helped Daddy make the bed for Grandma.
Mommy picked flowers in the garden,
and I made a "Welcome Grandma" sign.

Finally it was the day. Daddy brought Grandma
home from the airport. Mommy gave her a big hug.
I only watched.

Daddy said, "Don't you have a hug for your grandma?"
I shook my head. She looked like my Pat-a-Cake
Grandma, only different.

"Patta patta," she said.
She sounded like my Pat-a-Cake Grandma, only closer.

I wanted to say "Rolla rolla," but my mouth couldn't. I was too shy of this grandma. I played with Nosey and gave him kisses—nose kisses.

Mommy said, "Do you know who else likes that kind of kisses?"

I knew it was Grandma, but I only wanted to give them to Nosey.

"That's okay," Grandma said. She smiled at me.
I wanted to tell her something so I decided to
call Grandma on my telephone.
"Ding! Da-ding! Da-ding!"
"I think that must be for me," Grandma said.
"I wonder who it could be. Hello?"

"Patta patta," I said.

"Rolla rolla," said Grandma.

I said, "It's me, Grandma."

She said, "I'm so glad to hear your voice."

"I have to go now," I said.

My Pat-a-Cake Grandma was really there, right in our living room.

Nosey and I got the rhyme book.

"Well, look at this," Grandma said. "Maybe I'll read a bit.

"Hickety pickety, my black hen,
She lays eggs for gentlemen,
Sometimes nine and sometimes ten."

"Hickety pickety, my black hen." I whispered that part,
but I didn't say it loud.

"I know another rhyme," I said.

"Hark, hark, the dogs do bark,
My grandma is coming to town.
She'll fly in a great big airplane,
Up in the air and down."

Grandma laughed. "And here I am!" she said.

"I know," I said. "You are my real
  Pat-a-Cake Grandma."
"You bet I am," she said.
"Only something is different," I told her.
"What's that?" she said.
"Now," I said, "instead of O hugs,
  like in our letters, we can have real ones."
"And don't forget the kisses," said Grandma.

She gives my favorite kind.